WHO'S NEXT?

guess who!

First came the elephant with his friend, the lovely ladybug.

Guess who was next?

Tiger came next, with his friend the dog.

Who left?

Guess who
came next?

Owl came next, with a very friendly black cat.

Who left?

Guess who
came next?

Purple Dinosaur
came next,
with a funny
old tortoise.

Who left?

Guess who
came next?

Colorful Chameleon came next, with a little yellow duck.

Who left?

Guess who
came next?

Slippery Snail
came next,
with a beautiful
butterfly.

Who left?

Guess who came next?

Swishy Fish
came next,
with a hoppy
little frog.

Who left?

Guess who
came next?

Ginormous Giraffe came next, with a bouncy bunny.

Who left?

Guess who
came next?

Pink Piggy
came next, with
a teeny-weeny
little piglet.

Who left?

Guess who
came next?

Buzzy Bee came next,
with a tatty toucan.

Who left?

Guess who
came next?

A hungry horse
came next, with
a chirpy chicken.

Who left?

Guess who
came next?

A silly seal came next, with a scaredy spider.

Who left?

Guess who
came next?

A zigzag zebra
came next, with
Mischievous
Mouse.

Who left?

Guess who
came next?

A clever cow came next, with a curious crab.

Who left?

Guess who
came next?

A fierce crocodile
came next, with
a sleepy bird.

Who left?

Did you guess? Everyone did!

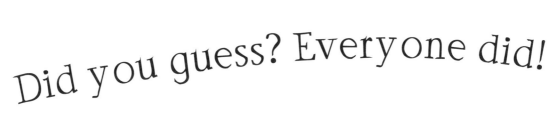

Who did you see?

Elephant

Seal

Butterfly

Pig

Zebra

Chicken

Chameleon

Giraffe

Ladybug

Dinosaur

Mouse

Snail

Bee

Toucan

Cow

Fish

Rabbit

Tiger

Spider

Piglet

Duck

Tortoise

Horse

Frog

Crab

Cat

Owl

Dog